Parents and Caregivers,

Stone Arch Readers are designed to provide enjoyable reading experiences, as well as opportunities to develop vocabulary, literacy skills, and comprehension. Here are a few ways to support your beginning reader:

- Talk with your child about the ideas addressed in the story.

- Discuss each illustration, mentioning the characters, where they are, and what they are doing.

- Read with expression, pointing to each word. You may want to read the whole story through and then revisit parts of the story to ensure that the meanings of words or phrases are understood.

- Talk about why the character did what he or she did and what your child would do in that situation.

- Help your child connect with characters and events in the story.

Remember, reading with your child should be fun, not forced. Each moment spent reading with your child is a priceless investment in his or her literacy life.

Gail Saunders-Smith, Ph.D.

STONE ARCH **READERS**

are published by Stone Arch Books
a Capstone Imprint
1710 Roe Crest Drive
North Mankato, Minnesota 56003
www.capstonepub.com

Printed in the United States of America in Eau Claire, Wisconsin.
030520
003316

Library of Congress Cataloging-in-Publication Data
Crow, Melinda Melton.
Drive along / by Melinda Melton Crow ; illustrated by Patrick Girouard.
p. cm. — (Stone Arch readers)
ISBN 978-1-4342-1866-7 (library binding : alk. paper)
ISBN 978-1-4342-2296-1 (pbk. : alk. paper)
[1. Trucks—Fiction.] I. Girouard, Patrick, ill. II. Title.
PZ7.C88536Dr 2010
[E]—dc22

                                        2009034289

Summary: Green Truck and Tow Truck play a game of follow the leader.

Art Director: Kay Fraser
Graphic Designer: Hilary Wacholz
Production Specialist: Michelle Biedscheid

Reading Consultants:
Gail Saunders-Smith, Ph.D.
Melinda Melton Crow, M.Ed.
Laurie K. Holland, Media Specialist

THE ROWDY RACCOON

Every time you turn the page,
look for the raccoon.

DRIVE ALONG

by Melinda Melton Crow

illustrated by Patrick Girouard

STONE ARCH BOOKS
a capstone imprint

This is Tow Truck.
This is Green Truck.

"I can go fast," says Green Truck.

7

"I can go fast, too," says
Tow Truck.

"I can go slow," says
Green Truck.

"I can go slow, too," says
Tow Truck.

"I can go in and out," says
Green Truck.

"I can go in and out, too,"
says Tow Truck.

"I can go up," says
Green Truck.

"I can go up, too," says
Tow Truck.

"I can go down," says
Green Truck.

"I can go down, too," says
Tow Truck.

"I can lift cans," says
Green Truck.

"I can lift you," says Tow Truck.

Green Truck and Tow Truck
can do different things.
They are good pals.

STORY WORDS

tow
fast
slow
lift
different
pals

Total Word Count: 114

Follow your favorite TRUCK pals as they learn about the open road.